ar out to sea you might notice something that looks like an island. It is constantly moving so you will not find it on any map. If you get too close (by boat or by plane) it will dive beneath the waves and disappear! You see, it's not an island. It's a gigantic turtle! (About the size of a football pitch). This turtle (called Morgana) is home to an entire village - with houses and shops - and even a park full of roses and small palm trees.

The people who live here are a cross between midgets and elves. They look like people, but have pointy ears (with tufts of hair) and furry tummies. They call themselves the Turtle People – and at the last count there were forty-seven of them.

Morgana is a very old turtle. Legend has it that she has been swimming around these waters since the age of the dinosaurs – and maybe even longer.

When the weather is good and the sea is calm, living on Morgana is easy. But when it is stormy and the waves are high, it would be quite dangerous and virtually impossible to live here – if it weren't for the fact that luckily enough Morgana has an extra shell – a green, transparent skin that she pulls over everything and everyone – a bit like pulling up the hood in a sports car. (It's the same when she dives, of course.) So each time the sky turns green, everyone knows that it's time to return to their homes and stay indoors for a while!

The people of Turtle Town live off fish. An ordinary-sized cod and two mackerel provide enough food for dinner for everyone. They collect rainwater in a clever system of gullies and containers.

The people of Turtle Town like trying to understand how everything works and what makes everything tick. This makes them a wise and inquisitive people, who like asking questions and enjoy finding new and surprising answers. However they also like sharing their answers with others – should anyone need help understanding anything …

Morgana is also home to Pix – the world's smallest master detective. This book is all about him.

Pix can talk to animals and birds – and fish too, of course. His greatest interest is all kinds of stories and myths. He also owns a magic dust that when sprinkled onto a figure of stone, plaster, wood or metal can bring it to life for almost a whole week!

PIX
and the troll hunt

by Tor Åge Bringsværd

Illustrated by Kjell E. Midthun

CHAPTER 1

What's become of The Scream?

The night watchman at the National Gallery in Oslo sits pensively eating his supper: one slice of bread with Jarlsberg cheese and one with brown goat's cheese. Suddenly he hears a rumpus over his head. A window smashes – and someone thuds across the floor. Meanwhile the burglar alarm goes off. The night watchman rushes upstairs. And raises his hands to his face in horror. Norway's most famous painting is no longer hanging in its place. (It's not hanging anywhere else either, for that matter.) It's been stolen!

The picture, called **The Scream**, was painted by the world-famous Norwegian artist **Edvard Munch**.
Although the police are working flat out, they have no idea who the thief is or where the picture has gone. Are there any clues? Only a gigantic woollen thread – two metres long and as thick as a fist!
No one can make head nor tail of it – so the newspapers report that the police are nothing but a flock of sheep. The whole thing is scandalous.

The mice in the gallery cellar agree - it is scandalous indeed. "Not a moment's peace to be had any more!" they complain to each other. "There are people with shiny buttons on their clothes running around here at all times of the day and night! And we used to have such lovely old canvases to chew!"
"If we don't want life to become completely impossible here, there's only one thing to do," says the oldest gallery mouse. "It's up to us to solve the case! And the sooner the better too!"
"Yes, but how?"
"We'll have to send word to Pix!" says Grandpa Mouse. "This is just the case for him!"

Northward bound

The following day a seagull arrives in Morgana. He lands in the park, very carefully, as everything in Morgana is frightfully small and he knows that this will make him seem extra large. When he spreads out his wings, he covers almost the whole of Turtle Town. The seagull is carrying a letter.
It is for Pix, the master detective – from the mice in Oslo. And it is quite brief. GET HERE QUICK! is all it says. Then there is a drawing of a map – so that Pix will know exactly where HERE is …

While Pix prepares for the journey, the people of Turtle Town make sure that the seagull (whose name is Hambro) has enough to eat. He has promised Pix a ride back to Norway.

Pix packs a small knapsack. In it he has all his detective's gear, including a small bag of magic dust. (If this dust is sprinkled on any figure of stone, wood or metal it will bring it to life for one whole day and one whole night – and sometimes for even longer!)
He bids farewell to his little chestnut tree and to all the tiny pot plants.
The lady who lives next door has promised to look after them.
Her name is Effi, and both she and Pix hope to become sweethearts one day. But they are both too shy to talk about it.

So Pix and Hambro the seagull set off northwards.
Hambro flies almost as high as the clouds. Pix holds on tight to the white bird's neck and nestles into the soft feathers enclosing him.

CHAPTER 3

On the trail

At last something other than sea emerges beneath them. At first they can see only lots and lots of small islands – but then the land itself rises up ahead of them. They fly inland over the Oslofjord. In front of them is Norway's capital city – surrounded by forests and hills.

Hambro flies over Bygdøy Island, right over **the Viking Ship Museum** and Thor Heyerdahl's **Kon-Tiki Museum**.

He swoops low over **Akershus Fortress** and **Stortinget**, the **Parliament building**, and banks steeply over the **Royal Palace** – because he wants Pix to see some of the city, he says – and then finally the big seagull lands safely on the roof of the National Gallery.

The mice have been scurrying around there for hours waiting for them.

Whilst Grandma Mouse brings out the cheese and biscuits, Grandpa Mouse explains all the dreadful things that have happened.

"But are you sure that there are no clues?" asks Pix.

"Only the gigantic woollen thread," says Grandpa Mouse. " Look! I made sure I bit off a little piece of it for you!"

Pix carefully studies the white thread. "And the police haven't found any fingerprints anywhere?"

"The thief must have used gloves," sighs Grandpa Mouse.

They sit right out on the edge of the roof.

Suddenly Pix points down below them. There, in the street, is a large hole just outside the art gallery.

"Nothing to worry about," laughs Grandpa Mouse. "Here in Oslo there are holes in the streets everywhere – and almost all year round too!"

But Pix shakes his head. "That is no ordinary hole," he says. "Can't you see what it looks like?"

All the small mice rush to the edge to have a look.

"Well I never!" squeaks Grandma Mouse and bites her own tail.

"It looks like a gigantic footprint!"But whoever can have such large feet?

CHAPTER 4

Big feet

This is without a doubt the work of a real troll," says Pix gravely, helping himself to another piece of cheese. "This will not be an easy case to solve, I'm afraid!"

"Troll?" shout all the small mice at once. "What on earth is a troll? Is it some sort of huge *cat*?"

"It's even more dangerous than that," says Grandpa Mouse. "But I didn't think they existed anymore … I thought they only belonged in fairy tales!" He looks down at the footprint in the street and shudders all the way to the tip of his tail.

Pix explains to the mice children what a troll is. He says they can also be called Jotuns and giants. He explains that they have lived in this country for thousands of years. In fact, they have lived inside mountains and under glaciers since long before humans settled here – they may even have been Norway's original inhabitants! Some of the giants are so huge that they can wade across large lakes. They often have two heads and some of them can take their hearts out of their bodies and hide them in clever places, before they go out to fight. (This also makes it almost impossible to beat them!) Pix says that trolls mostly emerge at night and during the twilight hours, because if the sun shines on them, many of them will simply burst and turn to stone. He goes on to say that apparently most trolls are extremely

ugly, although they do seem to have a lot of luck with princesses. Many stories tell of trolls living with princesses (or, at the very least, pretty girls), and even if it is said that the troll has stolen and kidnapped her, the girls do not always exactly seem to mind living inside the mountains …

The tiny mice children prick up their ears to listen. And a small mouse girl sighs longingly as Pix mentions princesses.

"But isn't it strange that there's only an imprint of *the left foot*?" says Grandpa Mouse, helping himself to the last piece of cheese. "Does he have a limp? Or is he *one-legged*?"

"The troll has used Seven Mile Boots," answers Pix. "I have never seen such boots myself, but they are well known in fairy tales. So if we travel seven miles in the direction of the footprint, we will no doubt find the imprint of the *right* foot as well!"

"You need someone who can help you," says Grandma Mouse. "Have you got anyone in mind?"

Pix nods. "I know just the right person for the job!" he says.

Thunder and lightning!

Pix waits until darkness falls, then makes his way down to **Oslo City Hall**. In the vast courtyard the walls are adorned with beautiful and colourful woodcarvings. Many of them feature scenes from the ancient Norse religion, which resisted Christianity until the year 1000 up here in the northern tip of the world. One of the pictures depicts the god of thunder. His name is Thor – or Thor and his Hammer, because the god of thunder always wielded a hammer as his weapon, a magic hammer that could break anything and anyone, that hit the slightest thing he aimed at and that always returned to his hand if he threw it at anyone. Thor rides in a chariot drawn by two goats. These goats are as much at ease on land as on water, but above all they like to fly!
Pix waits until there is no one around. Then he brings out his bag of magic dust. He takes a handful of dust and blows it at a carving with all his might.
"Baaaaahh!" say both the goats.

"Thunder and lightning!" bellows Thor. "Who do you think you are, you little pipsqueak? And why did you blow sand in my eyes?"

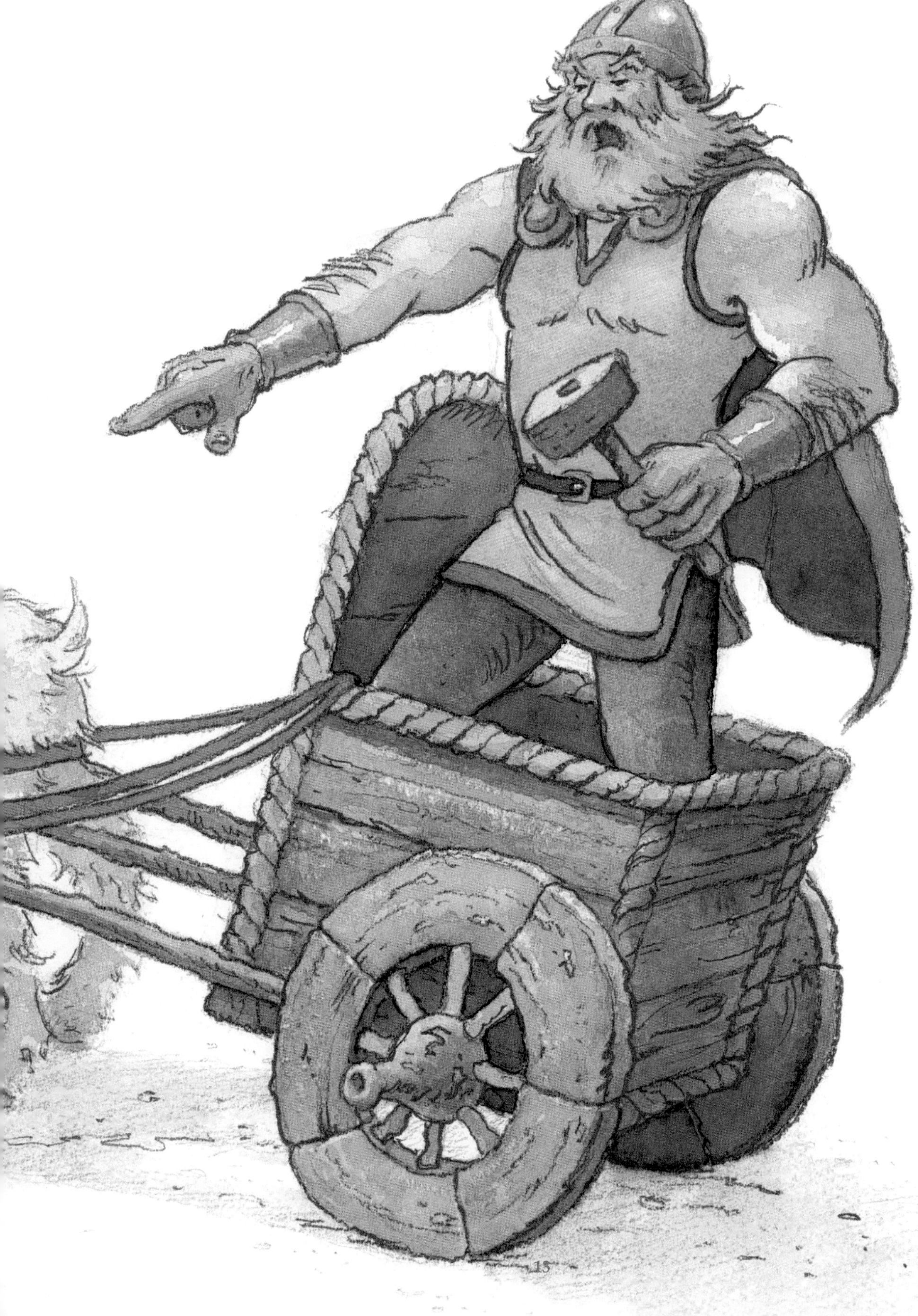

Pix hastens to explain. But Thor finds it difficult to understand. "Are you telling me I don't exist anymore?" he asks in astonishment. "But I'm standing here right in front of you!"

Pix explains that, thanks to the magic dust, the god of thunder will be allowed to live again – for one whole night and one whole day and maybe even a little bit longer. "And you may as well spend that time doing something useful," says Pix.

Thor isn't sure he can be bothered. If he only has a single day to live, he would rather be sitting in a pub drinking beer, he says – and maybe eating three or four pigs or such like. But when he hears that Pix needs his help to capture a *troll*, he pricks up his ears. You see, fighting trolls was always his favourite pastime. His shaggy red beard shakes in anticipation. "Jump in. My chariot awaits you, you rascal!" he roars. "We haven't a moment to lose!"

Thor giddy-ups his two goats, and the curious entourage swings up into the air, high above the houses and the streets. "Where are we off to?" the god of thunder bellows. "Eastwards? Northwards? I would usually find trolls in those parts in the good old days!"

"We must try and follow his tracks," Pix replies. The master detective uses his binoculars and scans eagerly in all directions.

There is a full moon.

The goats bleat happily at being let loose again.

"There might be something over there!" shouts Thor after a while. They fly low over the **Vigeland Sculpture Park**. "Look! Over by that little stone boy who looks so cross!" Well, well, if it isn't a new deep hollow – and the clear imprint of a right boot!

"I thought you said he was wearing Seven Mile Boots?" says the god of thunder. "It certainly isn't seven miles between these footprints." "He is probably out of practice," says Pix. "After all, it can't be easy keeping your balance with boots like those?" "I once borrowed a pair from my father," says Thor. "You see Odin, the king of the gods, liked all such fun and games. But I can

tell you it wasn't easy. I only meant to take a few steps, but I got completely lost. I couldn't find my way home again for several days!"
"I think this fellow is having problems as well," says Pix, "because I can see a new mark in my binoculars - on the hillside just up there!"
"Ah yes, **Holmenkollen**!" growls Thor. "A family of two-headed trolls used to live there in the old days. Maybe the thief is one of them – if they're still alive."
The footprint is close to **Holmenkoll ski-jump** – right outside the door to the **Ski Museum** (an impressive museum showing that Norwegians have been using skis for more than 4,000 years!)

The goat-drawn chariot lands next to the footprint because Pix wants to measure it – to try and work out how big the giant really is. Suddenly they hear a crashing in the forest right behind them.
A huge hulk of a troll appears.

Born with skis on their feet

The troll doesn't seem to notice them, because he is too busy picking flowers! Thor clutches his hammer and is about to pounce on the giant. But Pix holds him back. "We need an answer," he says. "And if you knock him out now, he will never be able to answer anything ever again!"

Although the troll has two heads (just as Thor said!), neither of his faces looks particularly dangerous. It is almost as if he is walking about smiling – with both his mouths. And the strangest thing of all is his feet. Pix had hoped to see Seven Mile Boots. But the troll has neither boots nor shoes on; instead, he is lumbering around with a large plank tied to each foot!

Now the troll discovers them.

He is so terrified that he drops the entire bunch of flowers. But then he frowns both his foreheads and rubs his four eyes. "Well I never," he exclaims. "If it isn't old Thor and his Hammer?"

"And by Jove, if it isn't you, Birger Holmenkoll!" blusters the god of thunder, because he has now had time to see who it is. The two of them are old acquaintances.

Once upon a time a long, long time ago they used to be enemies.

But that was when they were young and wild; now it suddenly seems pointless to fly at each other. Birger Holmenkoll says that he is the last of his family, the last surviving troll in the Oslo area. The rest of his family have

17

long since died and been turned to stone and moss. And the **Ekeberg Troll** – who lived in the hillside on the other side of town – burst over a hundred years ago.

Thor says that he too feels like a stranger in the world.

"You are welcome to come and live with me here," says Birger. "Then we could go flower-picking together …"

At this, the god of thunder roars with laughter. And the two goats bleat loudly, too.

Pix explains why they are there, and that they are searching for a troll who is wearing Seven Mile Boots. But Birger Holmenkoll says that he has been so busy looking for wood ane-mones and lily of the valley that he hasn't noticed anything at all. "My advice is that you look further west," he says. "Apparently there are more of our kind on the other side of the mountains."

Thor giddy-ups the goats again, and the chariot takes off from the ground.
The troll waves them off.

"I forgot to ask you why you're wearing a plank on each foot?" Pix shouts down to him. "They are skis, can't you tell?" Birger shouts back.

"But there isn't any snow here in the middle of summer."

"Well, all Norwegians are said to be born with skis on their feet – and we trolls want to show that we are as Norwegian as you can possibly be!"

"Does this mean you wear them all the time?"

"It has taken a little while to get used to it," Birger admits. "But now I wear them summer and winter, night and day – *yes, even in bed!*" Pix would like to ask more questions, but by now they are so far away from each other that the wind drowns out their voices.

"Not much trollishness left in that old heap!" grumbles the god of thunder. "Poor old Birger Holmenkoll, he's gone completely soft! It would almost have been better if I had used my hammer on him!"

It's *dripping*

I t is early in the morning. The sun has just risen. Thor and Pix fly as low as they dare, but don't really want anyone to notice them.
Occasionally they see something that might be a track. But they can't be sure.
"I only hope he hasn't tricked us!" says Thor. "In my day you could never trust troll rabble!" But Pix says that he feels it in his bones that they are on the right track. Anyway he has just spoken to two magpies that reckon they may have seen something enormous go past.

Are you sure it wasn't just a plane? Pix asks. Coo-coo, answer the magpies. (Which in magpie language means: *Do you think we're completely stupid, or what?*)

By the way, they come across plenty of planes. Once they nearly collide with one. The chariot almost hits the wing of the morning flight on its way to **Stavanger** – and any passengers who happen to be looking out of the window are left wide-eyed and staring.
But Pix knows that no one will believe them.

(Human beings are funny like that. They don't really believe in anything at all any more. Not if they can help it. And certainly not if it sounds odd..)

"Where are we actually?" asks Pix. He is trying to follow the map, but it isn't easy.
"We're in **Telemark**," Thor replies. "At this precise moment we are flying over a village called **Heddal**. But that funny-looking house down there… I have never seen that before."
"That must be **Heddal stave church** then!" shouts Pix. "I've read all about it. It is the largest of all the Norwegian stave churches. It's built of wood, but the oldest part is almost 900 years old! Let's make one more pass – so that we can see a bit more of it!" In his binoculars Pix is able to see that the portals have carvings of fabled animals and fantastic figures. He knows that inside there are more runic inscriptions – because that's how old this church is. (Runes were the letters used by Norwegians before they introduced the Latin alphabet they use today.)
"Isn't it a truly magnificent building?" says Pix.
"Well yes, it's not bad," answers Thor. "But for my part I like best the even older places of worship. The ones that were called hov, where people drank beer, sacrificed horsemeat and splashed blood on the walls!

There was usually a picture of me hanging on the wall as well!"
"Places like that don't exist any more," says Pix. "They were burned down when Christianity arrived in the country …"
The god of thunder doesn't say a word. He bites his lip and says
nothing.

Suddenly there is a strong gust of wind and a large spray of water hits them in the face.
"I can taste salt!" says Pix in surprise, licking his lips.
They look up, but there are no dark clouds to be seen, so it wasn't raindrops.
The goats bleat and wink at them. "Did you two notice that as well?" Pix asks (because he can talk to all animals and birds).
"Someone ran past us," says one of the goats. "Heading west!"
"And very fast!" says the other goat.
Pix licks his lips again. The taste of salt is still there. *Could it have been tears? It suddenly occurs to him. Was it the thief who rushed past us just now – with the Seven Mile Boots on his feet? But why is he weeping*?

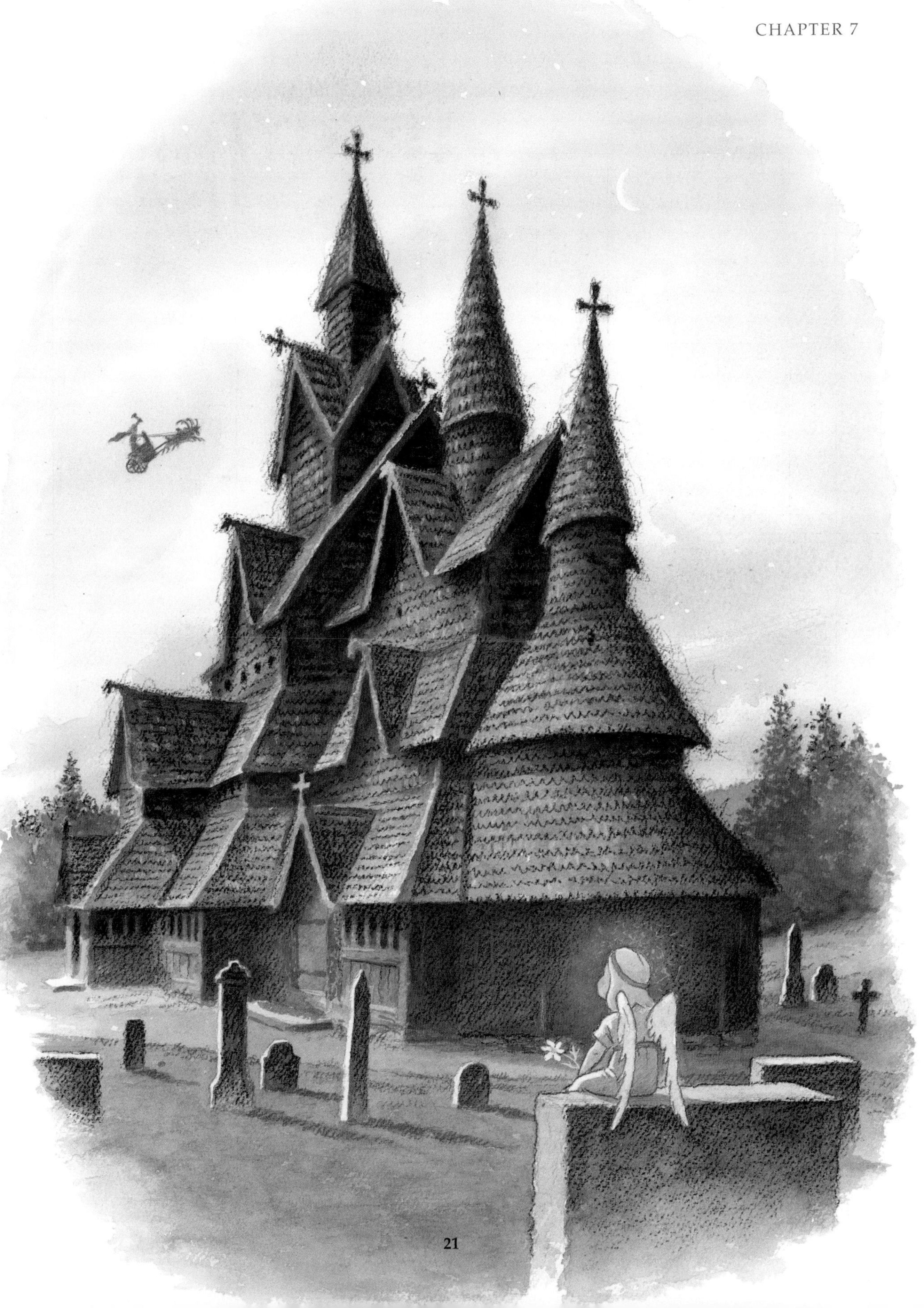

The barn pixies

Time for some food," says Thor. "And we'll do what I usually do, we'll find ourselves a nice farm …" He steers the chariot down to a rather isolated farm.

Pix leafs through his atlas. "I think this is **Morgedal**."

"It makes no difference to me what it's called, as long as they have something cold for me to drink!" mutters the god of thunder.

They land in the yard. The goats leave long skid marks in the gravel. But no one comes out of the houses to greet them.

"That's odd," says Thor. "In the old days the farmers would always appreciate a visit from me …"

Pix and Thor walk over to the front door and knock.

No-one answers.

They knock again.

"No-body lives here," says a thin, little voice.

"No-body lives here?"

"They've moved," says the reedy voice. "The people aren't here anymore. It's only us left now. And we'll be moving soon too, I expect."

"Don't play the fool with us," growls Thor.

"Come out so we can see you!"

A small grey-clad figure with a white beard jumps down from the roof. "I am the pixie on the farm here," he says. "You can call me Arnfinn, and I'm really a barn pixie. It's just that I no longer have a barn to look after. The people sold all the animals before they left. It's not easy being a farmer in Norway these days, I can tell you, and it's not easy being a pixie either!"

Arnfinn invites them into the empty barn where they meet his pixie wife and five barn pixie children. But Arnfinn says that they don't have much to offer their guests. A tin of fish balls is all they have, although they could always share it … and fortunately they have plenty of potatoes. But water is all they have to drink.

"I was hoping for a mouthful of beer," says Thor. "But I have never said no to a mug of fresh water either! And don't worry about food, because we have brought some with us."

"Have we?" says Pix surprised.

Without further ado Thor goes into the yard and wrings his two goats' necks. Then he begins skinning them.

The barn pixies and Pix cry out because this looks truly gruesome! But the god of thunder simply laughs. "It's not as bad as it looks," he shouts. "But when we eat them, we must remember to keep every tiny little bone. Not a single little knucklebone must go missing! And when we're all full up, I'll soon manage to bring my goats back to life!"

Arnfinn Barn Pixie stares at Thor. His eyes almost pop out of his head. "But that means you must ..." he begins. "That means you must be ..."

"I am Thor with his Hammer," says the god of thunder proudly, giving the small pixie a friendly nod. "And I'm mighty pleased that at least someone remembers me!"

They have an enjoyable breakfast. The goats are delicious and Thor eats a whole one himself, and at least half of the other one too. They talk about all sorts of things. The pixie family tell how nice it was to be barn pixies. They saw to it that everything on the farm ran smoothly. And as thanks the farmer would put out porridge for them. They tended the animals and were particularly fond of the horses. "But in the last few years there haven't been any horses here," says Arnfinn. "The farmer used a tractor instead. And it's just not the same patting and cuddling a tractor …"

There are still cats here though (which means there are probably mice too.) The five pixie children each sit with a pussycat of their own in their lap. Arnfinn smiles proudly when he looks at them. "It's been a good life," he says. "And Pixie Mother and I were hoping that our children would be able to take over from us. But now we will probably have to leave here together."
"Where are you thinking of going?" asks Pix. "I suppose we'll go into town, like everyone else," says Arnfinn sadly. "That will soon be the only place where there is work to be had. Maybe we can become factory pixies? Or look after a shopping centre? Who knows?"
"But we don't want to move, dad!" all the pixie children say in unison. "Because there is no-where else as lovely as here in Morgedal. Our village is famous all over the world!"
Pix nods. He already knows that Morgedal is called *"The birthplace of skiing"* and that it was here that the modern sport of skiing began, sometime in the 1850s. This is where the word *slalom* originated, for example. It is composed of *sla*, meaning slope, and *lom*, meaning tracks in the snow.
But when they mention the other tracks – the tracks that Pix and Thor are trying to follow –

there isn't much help to be had.
"You will just have to continue westwards," says Arnfinn shrugging his shoulders. "One way is probably as good as another!"

Thor has placed the goat hides next to the chariot where they have gathered knucklebones and all the other poor remains of the food. Then Thor swings his hammer over the goat hides, and, with that, the two goats spring to their feet again – as full of life as before!

Crazy girls!

They fly far and farther than far. To the very ocean itself. They travel far beyond **Stavanger**. Out in the North Sea they see huge, strange towers.

"They are oil platforms," says Pix. "Many people live and work out there, pumping oil up from the ocean floor!"

"Why don't these what-d'you-call-its drift off, like all other boats?" asks Thor.

"They are fastened to the seabed," replies Pix. "350 metres below the surface!"

"Have humans been doing this long?" Thor wonders. "Because in my day it certainly didn't look anything like this out here!"

"What is commonly known as the Norwegian gas and oil adventure began in 1969," Pix reads from a small guidebook (he never goes anywhere without a book like this which tells him everything about the country he is visiting). "It all began in a place called the *Ekko field*. In fact the entire coastline is divided into large fields and smaller areas called *blocks*. And they have quite funny names too! For example, the two largest gas fields are called *Troll* and *Heidrun*."

"Heidrun?" the goats bray. "We know all about her. She is the old goat who stands on the roof of *Valhalla* – back where we live in *Åsgard*, in the gods' world!"

"All day and all night scrumptious mead flows from her teats!" says Thor dreamily – because he is feeling thirsty again now.

Pix decides that they should turn back and go inland again.

"We won't find the thief out here," he says. "Although if we had more time, we might be able to find the Midgard Serpent," grumbles the god of thunder looking all around him. (The *Midgard Serpent* is the world's largest sea serpent. It is so enormous that it can coil itself around the whole world and bite its own tail. Old myths tell of fierce battles between Thor and his Hammer and this amazing serpent.) "We have a thief to catch," says Pix sternly. "And you have promised to help me!" "OK, OK, bossy boots!" sighs Thor and lets the chariot swing round to head inland again.

Over the **Lyse Fjord** Thor suddenly begins sniffing the air like a tracker dog. "I'm sure I can smell troll maidens?" he says. "Can you smell anything?" Pix shakes his head. "In the old days I used to be able to smell a troll maiden many miles away!" says the god of thunder. "And many of them were quite sweet too! Certainly not all monsters and old shrews! In fact I fathered children with one of them ..." (Pix knows the story of Thor and *Jarnsaxa* very well. They had a son, Magne, who was almost as strong as his father!) "Look over there!" Thor shouts suddenly. "I told you so!" He points to **the Pulpit Rock**, a steep cliff towering over 600 metres above the fjord. On the top is a large, flat plateau. And

up there ... well if it isn't two troll maidens standing there waving to them! Thor doesn't need to be asked twice. He lets the chariot land right next to the girls.

The troll girls look like humans, but are bigger – and they also have tails. Thor rubs his red beard and gives them a sly wink. But the girls are more interested in Pix. You see, they have never seen a tiny tot like him before. They grab his arms and throw him carefully to and fro between them like a ball. Surprised, Pix asks "But can trolls be outside at this time of the day? Aren't you afraid of the sunlight?" "You think we should burst and be turned to stone?" one of the girls laughs. "No danger of that happening when it's cloudy, like today. *Fair, partly cloudy weather*, they said on the radio!" The other girl hits her cheek to show that she has an earphone. "And we've got a walkman too, haven't we! We're always careful to listen to the weather forecast!" "Anyway, no-one is going to burst from a bit of sun," the first girl says. "But if you stay out in it too long, you can get pretty wrinkly!" And with that they burst out laughing again. "Do you girls live all by yourselves?" Thor asks suggestively.

"Only with our wolves and vipers!" the troll girls giggle. "You do know that we use wolves as our steeds and snakes as our reins don't you?"

Pix says that they will have to let go of him now. He is feeling slightly giddy from being tossed around like a ball. They put him down gently after first kissing him so much that his whole head is soaked.

The god of thunder is clearly envious. "Do you know who I am?" he roars suddenly.

The girls look at him mischievously, and curtsey politely.

"We know very well who you are," they say. "For grandma has told us all about you. She said that although you liked fighting her brothers, you used to treat our sort with *softer* caresses!"

Pix interrupts. "Unfortunately we don't have time for this sort of thing now!" he says, and clears his throat anxiously. "We are on the hunt for a thief. And we only have one day in which to find him!"

"I've been brought back to life by this little chappie here," Thor explains, stroking the two girls' cheeks. "But only for one day and one night apparently. And we have already used up the night!"

"So, then," says Pix. "Have you seen a troll pass by wearing Seven Mile Boots and carrying a painting under his arm?"

"Oh, yes!" the two girls reply in chorus. "And I can tell you he wasn't very steady on his feet! He was swaying to and fro over the fjord here for a while and then he disappeared again."

"Did you see which way he went?"

"Try in the direction towards Bergen," one of the girls says. And without saying another word, she runs straight over to the cliff edge and throws herself off!

"Don't be afraid!" the other girl laughs. "You see the backpacks we're wearing? Well, they are parachutes. We are into extreme sports; mountain climbing, deep-sea diving, hang-gliding, bungee jumping and parachuting. You have to have something to do. Otherwise it would be far too boring being a troll these days!" She waves to them and then she too jumps off **the Pulpit Rock**.

Pix and Thor walk carefully over to the edge and look down. Far below them two parachutes in all the colours of the rainbow are floating to the ground.

"But aren't you afraid that humans will see you?" Thor calls down to them.

"Only children can see trolls!" the girls shout back. "And hardly anyone believes what children say! So that's that!"

"I should have known!" Pix mutters to himself. Of course, that explains a lot of things. For example, why no one in Oslo saw the theft!

Troldhaugen

Pix and Thor follow the girls' advice and head for **Bergen**. Had they been normal tourists, there would be lots to see and do there. **Bergenhus Fortress** with "Håkonshallen", a banqueting hall which is over 700 years old, **Bryggen wharf** with its timber houses built in the old North German style, the famous **Fish Market** – and much more besides. But Pix and Thor are not on holiday. They are trying to track down a thief. And Pix has an idea where he might have hidden himself … On the outskirts of the town, near Nordåsvatnet Lake in Hop, is a place called **Troldhaugen**. The villa there was the home of *Edvard Grieg*, the world-famous composer who wrote the music to accompany *Henrik Ibsen*'s famous play about *Peer Gynt*, and there is surely

nowhere where there is more beautiful "troll music" than in that particular play!

The goat-drawn chariot lands gently in the park – close to the Grieg Museum.

The place is teeming with people who come here from all over the world. In the summer, "Troldsalen" is the venue for many popular concerts.

The tourists soon gather around the goat-drawn chariot and its two drivers. Pix has an idea. "Quick," he whispers to Thor. "*Say that we are making a film*! But say it loudly, so that everyone can hear."

Thor lets rip.

"We are making a …" he yells, but then he can't remember the rest.

"*Film*!" whispers Pix.

"We are making a film!" roars Thor, and his voice is so powerful that he blows the hats off the heads of the people standing nearby.

"Ah, yes!" the people say to each other. "So that's why. Now we understand why they look like that!"

"But how did they manage to appear straight out of the sky in a goat-drawn chariot?"

"Film stunts," comes the answer from various bystanders on the lawn. "Just stunts, of course."

Thor tugs Pix's arm. "What is a fi-fi… a whatever it was I said?"

"A film is a story told in moving pictures," replies Pix. "But everyone watching it knows that it isn't real."

"I don't feel particularly real, either," sighs Thor. "Not *particularly* …"

They sit down on the grass near to the "Composer's cabin". Edvard Grieg often sat here in this small log cabin when he was composing music. They are perfectly still. Because Pix has a hunch that they will soon hear something …

And sure enough, they soon make out a faint little tune. Someone is playing the fiddle. But where is the sound coming from? "SShhh!" Pix puts his ear to the ground. "He is sitting playing right underneath us!" he says.

Under a stone they find a handle – and a small door. But the entrance is far too small for Thor to be able to squeeze through. Pix will have to go it alone in here.

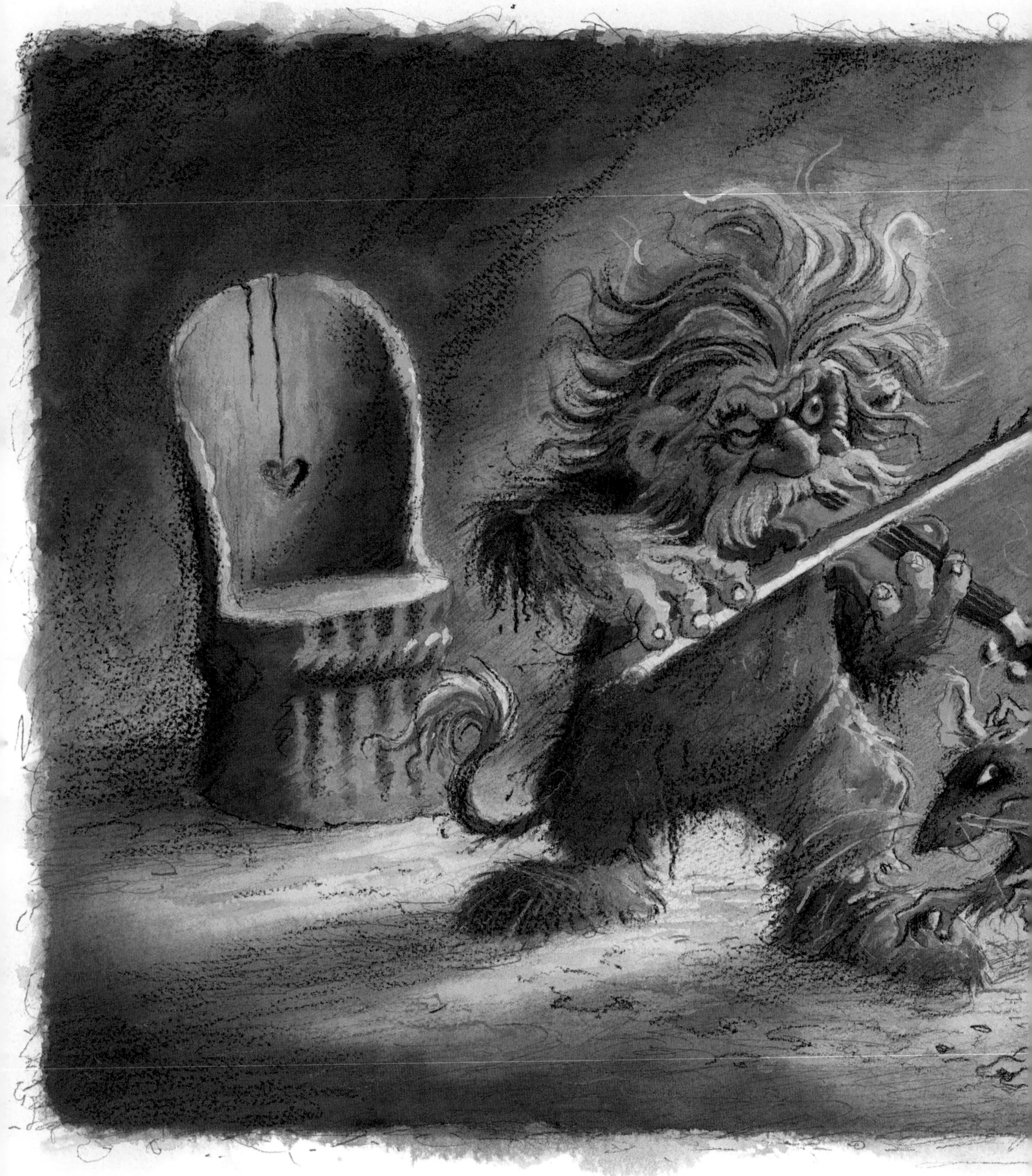

Dance, shouted the fiddle!

It is dark in there. But Pix gradually becomes accustomed to the dark. A narrow tunnel branches suddenly – and before he knows it he is standing in a room lit by burning candles. And this is where he finds the fiddler – a small troll with rumpled hair and a violin under his chin. He is standing on a chair. His eyes are closed and he is completely absorbed in what he is playing, so he doesn't notice Pix enter the room at all. In a ring around the troll sit four large rats listening, captivated. But when Pix coughs and says "Hello!" they turn around quickly and scratch the air in his direction.

"Ugh!" says the little troll looking up. "And just as I was in the middle of the trickiest bit!"

"Sorry to disturb you," says Pix. "But I am looking for –"

"Yes, I can well imagine who you are looking for!" the Fiddle Troll exclaims. "I know who you mean! Because he has clearly got a guilty conscience, and I knew straight away that people would be looking for him!"

"Has he been here?"

"Yes, well, not in here exactly!" The little troll laughs. "He was far too big for that. There's only room for us small trolls in here. You do know that there are trolls of all sizes don't you? And the one who was staggering around last night belongs to *the gigantic type* – actually they are quite rare, these days …"

"Staggering around?"

"Yes, he couldn't stand still for a single second in those silly boots. And the laces were knotted on one of them, so he couldn't take them off either!"

"Do you know who he was?"

"No. And even if I did, I wouldn't tell you. We trolls never snitch on each other!" The Fiddle Troll purses his lips and tries to look stern. "But he was hungry and I tried giving him some food. I sat on the lawn here, and held up cured hams high in the air – and each time he stormed past, he grabbed one. But he didn't make it easy for himself, because he was wearing large mittens! He could at least have taken them off."

Mittens! thinks Pix. So that's why there were no fingerprints in the National Gallery! The thief hadn't worn gloves, but mittens! And the woollen thread had of course come loose from one of the mittens!

An important piece of evidence if he ever managed to find the culprit!

The small troll explains that he is practising *Wedding March at Troldhaugen* by Edvard Grieg. Because he has been asked to be the fiddler at a wedding in **Lillehammer** this coming week. But it is a tricky piece, he says. So he really doesn't have time to stand around talking!

"Where did you learn to play so well?" asks Pix politely.

"From the water sprite who lives in **Vøringsfossen**," the troll replies proudly. "Maybe you could give him a message from me, if you are heading that way? Then I won't have to use one of my mail rats."

Pix looks at the rats in astonishment.

"Well, what did you think they were?" asks the troll. "Didn't you know that many of us still prefer to contact each other in the 'old way'? Of course, the youngsters use mobile phones and walkie talkies – but those of us who have lived a little longer have more trust in our mail rats!"

"And what message do you want me to give this water sprite?"

"Tell him that I will have to cancel my music lesson on Wednesday, because I'll be in Lillehammer at the wedding!"

Pix climbs out of the hole in the ground again. "Well?" says the god of thunder. "Did you find out where the thief has gone?"

Pix shakes his head. "Only that he has been here and run away again," he says.

CHAPTER 12

No one knows where the troll is!

The goat-drawn chariot takes off again from the park, and people stand waving excitedly to them. Thor and Pix wave back. "Where are we off to now?" asks the god of thunder.

"First we're going to stop at **Vøringsfossen Waterfall**," says Pix. "But after that I'm not sure ..." He thrusts out his arms dejectedly and flaps his ears sorrowfully.

They follow the beautiful **Hardanger Fjord** inland. At **Eidfjord** they turn up **Måbødalen Valley** before at last catching sight of the magnificent waterfall. **Vøringsfossen** has a total drop of 182 metres – and from the viewpoint at **Fossli Tourist Centre**, you can see the water plunge freely a full 145 metres straight into the chasm below.

On a large stone sits *The Water Sprite* right in the middle of the spray. He is playing his fiddle. But his music is drowned out by the roar of the waterfall. Pix and Thor try shouting down to him, but the old goblin neither sees nor hears them. "I don't dare to steer the chariot any closer than this!" says the god of thunder. At this, the goats bray and say that they are jolly glad too!

Then Pix has an idea. He writes the message from the Troldhaugen troll on a piece of paper, ties it to Thor's hammer – and lowers it down, right in front of the Water Sprite's nose.

It works! The Water Sprite stops playing, reads the note and looks up at them in amazement.

Pix raises the hammer again.

And without hesitating they continue on their way.

Behind them – down there on the slippery stone – the Water Sprite has already started playing again.

"Now I suggest we do as in the old days and head north and east!" growls Thor. "No-one knows where the troll is, so we may as well look in the places which used to be swarming with them in the old days!"

Northwards

They fly over **Jotunheimen** – Northern Europe's largest and most barren mountain region. Here they see Norway's highest peaks, **Galdhøpiggen** and **Glittertind**. However there are no traces of the troll to be seen anywhere …

"Northwards!" shouts Thor. "We will have to go further *north*!"

They fly over **Trondheim**. In the afternoon sun they see the light bounce off **Nidarosdomen**, the impressive cathedral where Norway's holy king, **Olav Haraldsson**, is buried.

"Just think if we could find another one of his rotten footprints!" grumbles the god of thunder, but he knows just as well as Pix that they are really searching in the dark. The thief may have gone this way, or he may just as well have taken another route altogether.

"But we will just have to enjoy all the things

there are to see," says Pix. "Because this is
certainly a beautiful country!"

Thor simply nods, and smiles into his beard.
He is thinking that he has been promised
only one night and one day – and maybe a
little bit longer. He knows that the further
north they travel, the longer the day will last!

"We are now crossing the **Arctic Circle**!" shouts Pix excitedly. He has his binoculars in one hand and his guidebook in the other. "Welcome to the **Land of the Midnight Sun**!" But suddenly he turns very serious. "Oh dear!" he says. "That thing with the sun ... we seem to have forgotten all about that!"

Because it is obvious that it isn't wise for trolls to live in Northern Norway. Even if they don't immediately burst from a little bit of sunshine, they definitely *don't* like it. And if a troll nevertheless chooses to settle here, it will also have to reckon on having to stay indoors – maybe even *sleep* – for the whole of the summer, a full six months. And who can be bothered to spend the summer like that?

"The winter and the polar nights are lovely" says Thor. "Because then everything is completely back to front!"
But Pix has made up his mind. "We are turning around," he says. "This is a waste of time. We won't find our thief either in **Lofoten** or at the **North Cape**. I can feel it in my ears!"

"Fair enough," says the god of thunder. "But we should take a little break first. My goats need to rest a little – and it would do them good to graze for half an hour or so."

Reindeers
know what they are talking about

They find a pleasant place to stop, far away from any people – a grassy plain covered with heather.

"You're a funny little chap," says Thor. "I wish we could spend more time together." He sighs. "But I don't suppose I'll last much longer?"

"Impossible to say," replies Pix. "Some last only a day, others can last a whole week..."

"Either way it's far too short," says the god of thunder. "Now that I've had a taste of life again." He twists his hammer in his hands. "But there's one thing I miss more than anything else," he sighs. "One thing I would really love to do before I disappear ..."

"And that is?"

"*I miss having a proper brawl,*" shouts Thor. "*I'm dying to thrust my hammer into the skull of a huge troll! Bang my head into its stomach! Give it a kick up the backside and send it flying into the mud!*"

"We have an agreement," says Pix.

"I know," sighs Thor. "I know that we have to ask and be polite. I know that the most important thing this time is to find the rascal who stole that painting. I know all that. But I must surely still be allowed to dream?"

"Dreaming is fine."

"But," says Thor rubbing his red beard happily. "When we have caught the scoundrel and retrieved the stolen goods ... and asked and been given an answer and all the rest of it ...

then surely I can teach this good-for-nothing a lesson or two? I mean: to make sure that he doesn't get up to more burglaries and nonsense?"

Pix laughs. But he doesn't have time to answer, because suddenly it's as if the entire plain comes alive!

A huge herd of reindeer storms up!

Pix is afraid of being trampled to the ground, but Thor stands in front of him, both feet firmly planted, his arms dangling by his sides like two huge clubs – it will take more than reindeer to topple a thunder god!

Luckily the animals avoid them.

But where are the two goats?

They hear a "Baa" right above their heads. Their two draught animals have chosen to seek refuge in the sky. Now they are skipping around up there.

The sight of the two air-borne goats causes the entire herd of reindeer to come to a halt – and Pix (who can speak all kinds of animal languages) hears that some of them are surprised and some of them are afraid, whilst others can only laugh.

"Goodness gracious me!" moos one of the largest reindeer. "Is that Father Christmas out practising?" The animal nods in the direction of the bearded god of thunder and laughs until his antlers shake.

"Who is Father Christmas?" bleat the goats to Thor in astonishment. "We don't know any Father Christmas!"

"Nor do we really," says the large reindeer. "But all the fairy tales say that he has a sleigh drawn across the sky by the likes of us – and certainly not by goats!"

A couple of the small calves nestle into Thor and look up at him admiringly. *"Are you really Father Christmas?"* they ask. "Do you think you would let us pull your sleigh when we are old enough?"

But now Pix intervenes. He explains to the reindeer that they are two detectives who are out on an important mission. They are trying to catch a thief – a large, dangerous troll. He tells them a bit about their experiences – and about how difficult it is to pursue someone who is wearing Seven Mile Boots.

"We've never met a troll," says the leader of the herd. "But now that you mention it, it did

45

once suddenly start raining – without there being a cloud in the sky … and the raindrops did taste salty – we experienced exactly the same thing."

"Where? When?" says Pix eagerly.

"Right over there and just a short while ago! We thought there was something a bit strange about the wind too. It was as if it blew right past us and then immediately came back again the other way!"

"That means he has been here too, and turned around again!" shouts Pix. "In that case we are back on his trail again! I bet we'll find the imprint of his boot not too far away – and that it points southwards!"

Thor hurries to hitch up the goats to the chariot again, and Pix climbs aboard. And sure enough … after only a few hundred metres they catch sight of a huge hollow – a clear mark of a left boot.

But why is he shedding tears? thinks Pix. *What kind of thief goes around weeping all the time?* The reindeer have followed them. They have run as fast as they can. Now they are standing in a circle around the big footprint catching their breath.

"Wait a minute," shouts one of the oldest reindeers and motions to them with his antlers.

"An old fairy tale has it that when Father Christmas is doubtful about something, he always consults *The Old Man of Fjærland*. Perhaps you too should go there?"

Pix thanks him for the tip – and Thor giddy-ups the goats.

On their way to **Fjærland** they also fly over **Geiranger**. "I've always liked this place," says Thor. "I've often taken a shower here – in the company of excitable troll maidens!" He points out one waterfall after another along the fjord. "That's **The Suitor** – that's **The Bridal Veil** – and that's **The Seven Sisters**!" Pix is impressed. No wonder this fjord is such a firm favourite with all sorts of cruise ships, he thinks to himself.

Then Thor also catches sight of the large boats. "By Jove, look!" he shouts. "Look at the size of them! And they haven't got any sails! How many men does it take to row such a whopper? A hundred? A thousand?" Thor has never seen a modern ship before, and wants to go down to take a closer look. But Pix shakes his head. They don't have time. They have almost run out of time completely! Instead he asks Thor to speed up the chariot!

The Book Troll

Færland is located deep in an arm of the Sogne Fjord (Northern Europe's longest and deepest fjord). Although it is only a small place, it has become known as "*Norway's book town*". There are many second-hand bookshops here and in mid-summer each year, there is a large book fair here. And since Fjærland stands next to Jostedalsbreen Glacier, a centre for glacier research has also been built here: The Norwegian Glacier Museum.

Evening falls as Pix and Thor slowly drift over the vast glacier and steer down towards the fjord.
They park away from the houses.
They make the last leg of the journey into **Fjærland** on foot. (That is, Pix sits in a bag that Thor carries over his shoulder.)

But where will they find the Old Man? And what does he look like?
They ask in several second-hand bookshops, but no one is able to tell them.

On the quay, Pix suddenly spies a large rat. It scurries off purposefully with a small post-bag on its back! It's a mail rat! Like the ones he saw at **Troldhaugen**!

Pix and Thor follow him. The rat stops in front of an unpainted wooden wall. He turns and rubs his rear against a knot at the lower end. Suddenly a door in the wall opens.

The rat slips in and the wall closes.
Pix and Thor press the knot too.
And follow him through the secret door.

They are standing in the messiest bookshop
Pix has ever seen (and he has seen quite a
few!). A small troll with glasses and a long,
crooked ear trumpet is sitting behind the
counter reading the letter that the rat has just
brought him.
The Book Troll looks up and politely greets
his new customers, and when Pix asks
whether he is the one they call *The Old Man*,
he nods and smiles. "And what can I do for
you?" he asks.
Pix says that they don't have time to buy

anything just now – although he loves rea-
ding. They need a different sort of assistance.
And then he recounts the whole story.
(It takes a bit longer than usual, because the
Old Man says "What?" all the time and puts
his ear trumpet to his mouth.)

"A ghastly story," says the Old Man finally.
"Shameful to hear that a troll could do such a
thing. The thief definitely deserves to be
caught. For hundreds of years, we trolls have
tried to behave as decently and quietly as we
possibly can, so that humans would forget
about us and not realise that we still exist –
and then this scallywag comes along and
ruins everything for us!" The Old Man is so

vexed that he almost breaks his ear trumpet.

But how are they going to find the crook? "You'll have to go to Lillehammer," says the Old Man. "There is going to be a large wedding there on Wednesday night. This is a message which I've just received from the groom." He brandishes the letter the rat has just delivered. "The bride and groom have asked me to hold the after-dinner speech!" Pix nods. He has already heard about that wedding.

"The whole family is going!" says the Old Man. "Every troll under the sun – which means that the thief is sure to be among the guests too!"

"Wednesday?" says Pix suddenly. "But that's tomorrow."
"What?" says the Old Man, suddenly busying himself. "Right, that means it's time to close the shop, pack my bags and get out of here! Good-bye to you both! Off you go!"

Wedding on Maihaugen

I don't like admitting it," sighs Thor. "But I seem to have taken a liking to these funny old creatures. After all, we are more or less related, the trolls and I ..."
"So you don't want to bash them on the head anymore?" smiles Pix.
"Far from it," growls the god of thunder. "It's just a question of finding one who really deserves it!"
"The thief perhaps?"
"He might just be the one, yes!" yells Thor swinging his hammer slightly.

The sun is setting as the goat-drawn chariot flies over **Mjøsa** – Norway's largest lake – and **Lillehammer** emerges ahead of them. This small town hosted The Winter Olympic Games in 1994 and is also home to **Maihaugen**, one of Northern Europe's largest outdoor museums, housing a collection of some 170 old buildings from the surrounding area and indeed the whole of the **Gudbrandsdalen valley**.

Pix and Thor know that this is where the troll wedding is due to take place.
It is a warm and tranquil summer's evening, and they land near an old summer mountain farm cabin with a grassy roof.

The museum has just closed, and the trolls are arriving in their droves. Some have one head, others have two or three – and some don't have a head at all, but carry it under their arms! Old men and women and unruly troll children. Many have decorated themselves with sprigs of spruce and most of them have tied a ribbon round their tails.
Pix and Thor lie in wait behind the cabin wall.
None of the wedding guests notices them. They see several trolls they recognise. Birger Holmenkoll is there, trudging around with his skis on his feet, as usual. The two troll maidens from the Lyse Fjord are doing acrobatic exercises on the grassy bank. And the little fiddler from Troldhaugen is sitting on a stone tuning his fiddle.

"I hope the Old Man of **Fjærland** makes it as well," whispers Thor. Then he checks himself. "I mean: I couldn't really care less! But he was a funny old fellow ..."

"But which one of these trolls is the thief?" mutters Pix. "How are we going to find the culprit?"

"Maybe he'll give the stolen painting as a wedding present?" says Thor.

They find the present table next to the old stave church. The table is loaded with presents – pots and pans, crockery, large, specially made sunglasses, a recipe book and an accordion, and even a stuffed moose head – but no Munch painting …

Maybe *The Scream* is lost forever? Pix thinks to himself. Perhaps this is a crime that will remain unsolved forever?

They hear loud, angry voices – and hurry to hide under the table. (There is barely room for Thor!)

It is the bride and groom arriving – and they are arguing like cat and dog, *even before they have got married*!

The groom is a huge hulk of a troll, but the bride – Pix nearly has to blink three times – the bride is a human, a young girl with a tiara on her head!

"OK, OK, OK!" she says stamping her foot. "I admit that I'm not a real princess, but there jolly well aren't many of those around these days either! And you were surely not so stupid as to think that you could get hold of one simply by placing a personal ad in the paper?!"

"I put: *Troll seeks marriage with princess*," grumbles the troll. "And that was exactly what I meant!"

Suddenly the bride turns softer and friendlier.

"But we're as bad as one another really, aren't we?" she says, stroking the troll's stomach. "Because you jolly well tricked me too!"

"Did I trick you?" It is obvious that he likes being stroked.

"Yes, after all, I never in a million years thought that you would be a real troll," she smiles.

"I thought it was just someone being funny! So in a way *I* was tricked too!" She smiles at him. "And *you* were tricked because I am not a real princess – even though I once won a beauty contest in Hønefoss, and that's the whole truth …"

"Carry on stroking!" commands the troll. "You're good at it. My tummy likes it!" He puts his arm around her. "And if we really have tricked each other, both of us … well then –"

"Well then, we'll just have to make the most of it," says the girl. "And in any case it's true that I always wanted a huge boyfriend! Although I never dreamt that I would find anyone as huge as you!"

"The bigger the better!" laughs the troll.
And then they kiss one another!

At this precise moment Pix has to sneeze. The bride and groom look under the present table in amazement and discover them.

"Who on earth are you hiding from?" asks the groom. "Are you guests, by the way?" He turns to the bride. "Maybe they're from *your* family?" But the girl shakes her head. "None of mine are coming," she says sadly. "There was no point even asking them. Because I know they would only have said *no*!"

"As we're talking about guests," Pix interrupts hurriedly. "Do you know if they've all arrived yet?"

He explains why he is asking. And the bride and groom listen with interest. Oh yes, they have heard about the theft from the **National Gallery**.

"And all the trolls from the whole of Norway are here at Maihaugen at this very moment?" Pix repeats the question.

"I know of at least two who are missing," says the groom reluctantly. "One is the Old Man of **Fjærland** – although he nearly always turns up at the last minute …"

"And the other?"

"I have a cousin in **Rondeslottet**. I've sent mail rat after mail rat to him, but he hasn't replied once. Perhaps he doesn't live there any more? I know he was talking about moving to **Hunderfossen waterfall**. After Aunty passed away recently – that's his mother – poor Guttorm hasn't been quite the same …

For example, people say that he wears mittens all the time, even in the middle of summer!"

"Mittens?"

"Yes, because his mother knitted them for him – so I guess it's a way of remembering her …"

Pix and Thor give each other a look as if to say "We've got him". Now we know who the thief is at last!

Inside the mountain

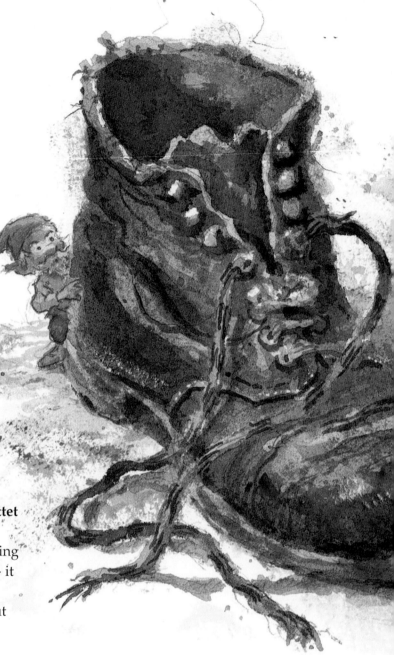

First they fly to Hunderfossen waterfall, as it is only a few minutes away. There is a large family park here – a proper theme park for adults and children alike. And there are many reminders of trolls here, a 14 metre tall statue of a troll guards the entrance to a fairy tale grotto and there is even a "troll restaurant" … but even so, Pix believes that there are probably a few too many people in the park for cousin Guttorm to want to live there.

So they go to **Rondane**, the famous mountain area that in 1962 became *Norway's very first National Park*, and which through the years has provided the inspiration for many authors, composers – and above all painters.
"Look over there!" says Pix pointing up.
"There's the mountain they call **Rondeslottet** – I recognise it from a picture I saw in the National Gallery in Oslo, when I was looking for clues, called *Winter's Night in Rondane* - it was painted by someone called Harald Sohlberg. And in Henrik Ibsen's play about *Peer Gynt*, this is precisely where the troll king himself lives!"

Night has now fallen. But Norwegian summer nights are light. So it is easy to find your way about.
They land at the foot of the mountain, just in front of a steep cliff.
"But where's the door?" says Thor. "And how are we going to get in?"
"Well, I doubt the person who lives here has a doorbell," smiles Pix.
But what is that scurrying across the heather just over there?
Two large mail rats! And four more!

showing where their front door is. They only want guests who can find their own way.) Just inside the door are the Seven Mile Boots, dirty and muddy from all the leaping about – almost the length and breadth of the entire country!

The rats notice that someone has followed them in, so they wait. "Who are you, and what do you want?" they hiss. "We just want to say hello to the person who lives here," answers Pix politely in rat language. "And we bring greetings from his cousin in **Lillehammer**." The rats clearly relax, and the largest of them sighs heavily. "Greetings, indeed!" he says. "We have been bringing so many letters here, that we have lost count altogether! But he can't even be bothered to read them! Just looks sadly at the envelopes and throws them on the fire! Can't understand how anyone can be bothered to carry on writing to him!"

"Who is that blathering away out there?" bellows a deep voice suddenly. "Is it those stupid wedding invitations again? Can't I be left in peace?"
"There you are!" says the largest rat. "He's completely *impossible*!"

And they are heading straight for a crevice in the mountain.
"Come on!" says Pix. "Let's follow them!"

The crevice is not as small as it looks, in fact it is a lot bigger – undoubtedly troll magic has made it look so narrow …(Trolls don't like

CHAPTER 18

The culprit

Guttorm sits by the fire with both his heads in his hands. On a small ledge right in front of him is the stolen painting.

"Is it OK for me to bash him on the head?" whispers Thor eagerly.

But Pix holds him back. "Surely we have to find out a bit more first?" he says.

"More?" thunders the god of thunder.

"There's the picture. There's the thief. What more do we need to know?"

"For example, Why!" says Pix.

"Don't stand there whispering!" roars Guttorm. He signals for them to come closer, and Pix and Thor slowly approach the glow of the fire.

"Lovely mittens you've got," says Pix. (Because Guttorm is wearing them even in here!)

"Real *Selbu mittens*!" says Guttorm proudly. "The best mittens in the land! Mum knitted *them for me. She wanted to knit me a Selbu sweater* as well – but that's when it all happened …"

"Tell!"

"She wanted to go out for some more wool," says Guttorm. "And she thought it was going to rain all day. She was so excited that she forgot to listen to the weather forecast. Just over by Dovre she was surprised by the bright sunlight. Old as she was, she burst immediately. Into a thousand pieces!" Guttorm wipes away a tear from the corner of his eye.

"You were very fond of her, weren't you?"

"Fond?" roars Guttorm. "She was my mother!" And then he weeps so much his tears splash across the whole floor.

"There, there," says Thor, because he always gets a bit upset when he sees that someone is unhappy. And he doesn't think it is particularly heroic to crack someone's head open when he is weeping – even if it is a troll.

"But you are aware that you have committed a serious crime?" says Pix. He goes right over to Guttorm and looks sternly into his huge tearful eyes.

"Of course I'm aware of that," sniffs Guttorm. "But I had to! Just had to! I just *had to have* that picture!"

"*Had to?*" Pix shakes his head perplexed.

"Well just look at it!" wails the troll. "Isn't she wonderful?"

Pix and Thor look at the screaming figure in the picture, but "wonderful" certainly isn't the first word that springs to mind.

"And she looks just like her!" howls Guttorm. He leans forward and strokes the picture tenderly.

Pix and Thor still do not understand what the troll means.

"*She looks just like my mother!*" shrieks Guttorm. "And when I heard about that picture … and when I saw it … I knew I had to have it. Because then I would somehow have my mother here after all – even if she's dead!" He gets up and lifts the picture up.

"I thought it might hang above the fire? Or can you see somewhere else here more suitable?" Guttorm gazes at them with his large, eager eyes.

The end?

It isn't easy getting Guttorm to understand that the painting has to be returned to the National Gallery. "They have so many pictures," he cries. "A whole house full! And I only want this one!" But, in the end, he realises that he has to give it up. Especially when Thor starts agitating …

Both Thor and Pix feel sorry for the poor troll and try their best to cheer him up. Pix promises that they won't tell anyone who the thief was. Because, after all, the most important thing is to hang the famous painting back in its place. Thor suggests that he and Guttorm have an arm-wrestle, "because there's nothing more likely to put you in a good mood than testing your strength!" he reckons.
The troll agrees! It turns out that they are almost as strong as each other …

All three of them have a jolly good time for quite a long while. Guttorm brings out huge barrels of beer for himself and Thor – and roasts two pigs as a midnight snack.

But just before sunrise, it all ends.
Pix and Thor take the picture with them, and leave **Rondeslottet**.
Guttorm stands in the mountain crevice waving to them with a large red handkerchief – and they can clearly hear that he has started weeping again.

So it's off to Oslo again. They want to make it to the National Gallery before daylight dawns completely.

They land on the roof of the building. Grandpa Mouse has been sitting there patiently waiting for them. And he and the other mice help Pix to hang the picture back in its place again – without the watchmen noticing. Mission accomplished!
But what about Thor? Will the god of thunder soon disappear and once again become a shadowy dream – as he has been for the past one thousand years?
How long will he last? How many days and nights has he got left?

Thor and Pix look at each other. "Do you regret that I brought you back to life for this short while only?" says Pix.
The god of thunder shakes his head. "It's been great – both for the goats, and me" he replies. "We're not complaining. Even though hardly anything was as I had expected."
"What were you expecting?"
"I thought I was going to get to fight trolls again!" says Thor. "But instead I have almost become *friends* with them!"
"Maybe you aren't so different after all?" smiles Pix.
"Precisely!" answers the god of thunder. "We are of ancient stock. We are of those who

mostly belong in legends and fairy tales! And now I'm going back to **Rondeslottet**. I want to spend the time I have left with Guttorm. We can arm-wrestle and drink beer, and tell each other tales from a world we both remember, but which no longer exists ..."

They bid each other farewell. The goats lick Pix's face and bleat good-bye. And Thor gives him a beardy hug. But before Thor leaves, Pix gives him a large roll of paper. "It's a poster," he says. "A copy of the picture Guttorm likes so much. You can take it to him – so he can hang a picture of his mother on the wall after all!"

Pix and the mice stand on the roof waving until they can no longer see the flying goat-drawn chariot. "Who knows how long you will last, old thunder god," Pix mutters to himself. "But maybe you will live forever – in there inside the mountain."

The little master detective feels his heart-strings being tugged as he stands there waving. So he asks Grandpa Mouse to send for the large seagull straight away. He is going to fly him back over the ocean and home to Morgana – as they had agreed. Because everyone misses home when they have been away for a while.
Even master detectives.

THE END!

Publisher
Terrascope Publishing as
Post Box 388
N-1323 Høvik

Telephone +47 22 36 06 70
Fax +47 85 03 41 61
E-mail mail@terrascope.no
www.terrascope.no

Author: Tor Åge Bringsværd, Norway
Illustrator: Kjell E. Midthun, Norway
Translation: ComText as, Norway

Design: Filius Design as/Kristin Stephansen-Smith, Norway
Repro: Capella Media as, Norway
Printed by Nørhaven A/S, Denmark
Photo page 7: J.Lathion, © Nasjonalgalleriet